Flamenco Fantasy

Written by Cynthia Ventrola Struven

Illustrated by Beverly Womack

Dedication:

To my mother, Cathy Ventrola,
who danced with us around our
living room to clapping, castanets, and
music from the album, *Soul of Spain.*
—CVS

Dedicated to my granddaughter,
Beatriz, the tiny dancer.
—BW

"I hope I don't fall off the stage and break my leg," said my best friend, Jessica.

"I hope I don't daydream and miss my cue – or forget my routine," I added. I smoothed the ruffles of my dress with clammy hands.

Jessica and I linked arms and we strolled through the dressing rooms. The backstage buzzed with the chitchat of contestants ages nine to twenty-one. Our knees trembled. Our smiles quivered. Our stomachs tumbled. Auditions for the Junior and Senior Spirits of Fiesta had finally arrived!

"You'll never win," said our classmate, Dolores. She flicked her tongue in and out like a snake and glided past us. Our smiles flip-flopped into frowns.

"She *is* pretty," admitted Jessica.

"She *is* a good dancer," I added.

"She better not let the judges see something like that," whispered Blanca, one of the older girls. "Junior and Senior Spirits of Fiesta need to be friendly. They never tire of smiling at audiences during Old Spanish Days© – or of comforting the beginning dancers!"

I peeked around the stage curtain. Sure enough, four judges sat on the balcony ready to examine us through their binoculars and then score our dance routine. Old Spanish Days© officials, relatives, and Flamenco *aficionados* were filing into the theater.

Worries nagged me. Had I kept all the rules? Would I keep my friends—whether or not I won? Was I from the "right" family?

My ancestors were not *Presidio Comandantes, Rancho Don*—or even California citizens.

My family works and lives on a ranch in the coastal hills of Santa Barbara. Like generations of other California families, my parents migrated from Mexico to provide us with the necessities of life—and an education. Their encouragement inspires me to strive for my best, to pursue my Flamenco passion, and to make them proud.

I watched *Mamá y Papá* from the stage. Though unable to speak English, they sat ready to cheer for me! They had washed and ironed their tattered clothes. They had scrubbed away the stains from their strong, calloused hands. They sat up straight in the theater seats, smiling but bashful, their hands clenched in their laps.

"The show starts in five minutes," the monitor called. "It's time to line up for the Promenade of Participants."

One at a time we danced for mere seconds before the audience. When my turn came up, I spun across the stage like a top, pulled along by the music.

The master of ceremonies appeared at the microphone to announce the first contestant: my best friend Jessica.

She moved onstage, dancing to the beat of the song "Aire." She rolled her shawl on an imaginary wind. The shawl curled like a tumbling wave of the sea.

"She looks just like a Gypsy dancer of long ago," I thought. And then I imagined what my life would be like as a ten-year-old girl in another time and another place...

The year is 1490.
Night has descended on Andalucía, Spain.

I am a Gypsy girl, and our community of nine families gathers round a campfire. Clapping, snapping and shouting liven the enclosure made by our wagons. The horses stomp their hooves and nod their approval. Our dog performs a tail-chasing dance.

My father sits atop a boulder. He thumps his guitar and releases his emotions. The buckles on his shoes and the gold-coin buttons on his vest twinkle, reflecting the firelight. The ends of his shabby bandana bob with the beat of his song of distress. His hoarse voice wails his *duende*—the anguish that drives and inspires him. He recounts his wanderings. He recalls his toil and poverty. He weeps over society's cruelties. He sows his words into the wind, and they scatter like seeds into the hearts of the sympathetic listeners.

My mother weaves a dance around the fire like a spider spinning her web. She works her scarves like willow trees waving their branches. Bracelets wiggle and tinkle on her wrists. Earrings jiggle and twinkle in her ears.

She beckons me with her free hand. I jump into the clearing and flutter my skirts like a bird ruffling its feathers. A hot wind blows across the Guadalquivir Basin and whips my ragged dress. I move with the wind and music, imagining myself a dust devil spinning across the desert.

This was how I learned to dance..

Jessica's performance ended and I snapped out of my daydream. I squeezed her hand and smiled at her when she returned to her seat. The Master of Ceremonies announced the next participant: Giovanni, the son of my dance teacher. His mother was a former Spirit of *Fiesta*—so he was born dancing!

He began his routine sitting in a chair with his back to us, hands on his hips. He slipped a red cape off his shoulders and spun it round his head. He fanned it before an imaginary bull then tossed it aside. Slowly rising to a standing position, his black boots drummed the floor to the lively beat of the song. Giovanni revealed a baton. He moved with it as with a dance partner—guiding it, guarding it, embracing it.

The sway of his baton hypnotized me. I imagined myself as a student in another time and another place...

The year is 1862.
A heat wave assaults Triana, Spain.

I am a student attending an *Academia de Baile*, a school dedicated to teaching Flamenco dance. Here I exercise to strengthen my muscles. I train to coordinate the placement of my arms, body, and legs. I practice hand movements, turns, and finally footwork. I learn to recognize the different musical rhythms. Night and day, I soak in Flamenco. It is poetry in motion! I want to capture its passions: joy and despair, love and rejection, liberty and tyranny.

I hear about the famous Flamenco singer, Silverio Franconetti. Perhaps he will notice me. Maybe he will invite me to perform at his popular *café cantante*!

Our instructor frowns. Then he reprimands us.

"Your posture imitates flowers wilting in the sun. Flamenco is a stretching heavenward! It is a reaching for freedom!"

"Carina Cruz will be dancing..."

I toppled out of my fantasy when the Master of Ceremonies called my name. My heart leapt into my throat!

Jessica clutched my arm. "Good luck," she whispered.

The stage manager hustled me to the curtain.

I stepped out to face my audience. For a moment I felt paralyzed. But when the music began, the magic began. It pulsed like electricity through my body. It energized and excited me. It was the puppeteer and I the puppet.

While I danced I imagined myself as a Flamenco dancer of another time and place...

The year is 1876. A full moon shines upon the famous Café Silverio in Seville, Spain.

I am sixteen-year-old Juana Vargas, La Macarrona. On a raised, wooden platform I perform a *baile intermedio*—a light and not so serious dance. Besides me, our *Cuadro Flamenco* consists of a singer, a guitarist, and a *jaleador*. They rally me with shouting, snapping, and clapping. The music echoes around the pillars and through the carved arches enclosing the patio. It soars to the guests seated at tables up in the gallery. I raise my arms in a graceful arch and flutter my hands like butterflies.

My partner Miracielo joins me on the stage. He performs his *baile chico* — a joyful, energetic dance. I reduce my dancing to the cobra-like movement of arms and hands. Fire blazes from my dark eyes. I tease Miracielo using my castanets. He argues back with his heel-stomping *zapateado*. The tapping of his nail-studded shoes reminds me of a blacksmith hammering at his anvil. Our performance ends. We bow to the spectators who erupt into applause...

I draped my skirts over one arm, and waved with the other as I moved offstage. The applause thrilled me and I felt a blush spread up into my face as I settled into my seat. I looked around then. Dolores stared at me, her mouth hanging open. Had I messed up?

Then the Master of Ceremonies called Dolores's name. Dolores started her performance. She skipped around the stage and threw imaginary flowers from the hat in the crook of her arm.

Jessica jabbed me with her elbow to make sure I paid attention. But I was already thinking about a performer in another time and place. I could only wonder what she would have felt and thought...

**The year is 1949.
A clear, blue sky hangs above
Santa Barbara, California.**

I am Lia Parker,   the first Spirit
of Fiesta.   I wait on the steps of
Mission Santa Barbara. Today is
La Fiesta Pequeña,   the opening
ceremony of the city's week-long
celebration of its Spanish
heritage.

As Spirit of Fiesta, it is my duty
to help preserve that.

I recall all that occurred to make it possible for me to stand at the front door of the Queen of the Missions: Franciscan *Padres* from Spain established her; Chumash Native Americans built her; Spanish soldiers guarded her.

A Franciscan Friar blesses Old Spanish Days©. I start my Spanish dance. The festivities have officially begun.

I pulled out of my daydream when Dolores finished her routine. After an imaginary trumpet flourish she returned to her seat with her nose in the air. *She is a good dancer,* I thought.

Sixteen more dancers needed to audition. It would be a long wait before *El Presidente* revealed the winner.

****

An hour and a half later, last year's Junior and Senior Spirits made their speeches and performed their farewell dances. The Master of Ceremonies called all the participants to line up on stage. Our stomachs somersaulted: the verdict had arrived.

"The runner-up for Junior Spirit of Fiesta is.... Giovanni Farruco!"

We applauded generously, glad for our friend. But hope seemed to be fading away for me, like the sun dipping below the horizon. One more announcement remained. I fidgeted. I twisted my dress in my hands.

"And the winner is....Carina Cruz!"

I screamed and my hands flew to my face. Jessica embraced me. Last year's Junior Spirit of Fiesta handed me a bouquet of flowers. Tears mixed with make-up slid down my cheeks and I quickly wiped away the evidence that this was no fantasy. I noticed Dolores turn away, attempting to wipe tears from her own eyes.

"It was your passion," said Jessica.

"It was your grace," said Giovanni.

"It *is* a land of opportunity," Mamá said in Spanish.

The clock atop the Santa Barbara Courthouse announces ten o'clock on a bright Saturday morning in August. It's time for the Senior Spirit of Fiesta and me to lead the way! The children's parade, called *El Defile de los Niños*, marches onto State Street.

The cheers of the twenty thousand spectators who line the parade route send a shiver up my spine. A cold lump sinks into my stomach when I notice the sea of faces watching me. I search for my family in the crowd. When I finally spot them my fears drift like the sailboats in the harbor.

I try to take it all in. Child vendors weave in and out among the crowds selling decorated headbands and confetti-filled eggs called *cascarones*. Flower girls throw petals from their baskets. A swarm of children trail us dressed in traditional Old Spanish Days© costumes. Papier-mâché bullheads disguise others, and they zigzag after their prey mocking a "Run with the Bulls."

Flamenco, Mexican Folk Dance, Salsa, and Ballet dance studios entertain the crowds. Junior-sized mariachi bands and school bands perform their versions of songs like "Macarena" and "Malagueña." Floats depicting episodes of California History crawl along the course. Equestrians on decorated horses bring up the rear of the parade.

A newspaper reporter interviews me after the parade.

"What do you like best about Old Spanish Days©, Carina?"

"Dancing Flamenco! I feel so alive when I dance—and I want others to feel its excitement! The history of Flamenco reminds us that if we learn from the difficulties of our past we can make a better future." I throw my hand into the air. *"Viva la fiesta y viva la familia! Olé!"*

Vocabulary

Academia de Baile: dance academy

Aficionados: people enthusiastic about a particular thing

Aire y Gracia: light and graceful

Baile Chico : a dance characterized by joyful and lively dancing with rapid footwork and arm movements

Baile Grande: a slower and more serious dance

Baile Intermedio: contains some of the same elements as baile grande but is lighter

Bulería: dance that runs to the beat of a song

Café Cantante: a café where Flamenco is performed

Cantaor, Cantaora: gypsy singer (male, female)

Cante Chico: lighter and brighter gypsy song

Cante Grande: a gypsy song expressing anguish

Cante Hondo: 'deep song'; general heading for the purest and most serious gypsy song

Cante Intermedio: gypsy song in between *Chico* and *Grande* in intensity

Cascarones: Decorated, hollowed eggs filled with confetti

Comandante: commander

Cómpases: a measure of musical composition (There are the four-count *compáses* of *taranto, rumba, farruca, tango and zambra.* There are the twelve-count *compáses* of *soleares, bulerías, and alegrías.*)

Cuadro Flamenco: the four parts of a Flamenco performance: dancers, singers, guitarists and jaleodores

Desfile de los Niños: Children's Parade

Duende: an inner drive or inspiration to perform the Flamenco tradition

Familia: family

Fiesta: party

Fiesta Pequeña: Little Party; in this instance, the Old Spanish Days© opening ceremony

Kumpania: a group of gypsy families that traveled together

Jaleodores: people who provide the clapping, snapping and shouting in support of the singers, dancers, and guitarists in a Flamenco performance.

Mamá* y *Papá mommy and daddy

Mariachi Band: a musical group that performs Mexican Folk Music. The instruments may include violins, trumpets, a vihuela, a guitarrón and one or more guitars. The guitarrón is a large bass guitar-like instrument with six strings and a large belly in the back. The vihuela is a small guitar variant also with a belly and five treble strings.

¡Olé!: Bravo!

Padres: parents

Padre: Father or Priest

Pitos: snapping

Presidio: fort

Rancho Don: owner of a large Spanish land grant

Silverio Franconetti: (Spain June 10, 1831 – May 30, 1889) Flamenco Singer who owned the "Café de Silverio" to which he invited the most excellent Flamenco figures of that Golden Age of Flamenco.

Senior and Junior Spirits of Fiesta: Title of the two girls who embody "the gaiety and vitality of Santa Barbara's annual summer festival. She has come to be the visual representation of Fiesta, a goodwill ambassador to local residents and visitors alike during the annual Old Spanish Days© festivities in Santa Barbara, California." (Old Spanish Days© webpage) The girls are awarded the title after winning a dance competition in their age category.

Toque de Palmas: Clapping

Vardos: wagons or tent dwellings of the gypsies

Zapateado: footwork in which the feet drum the floor

Viva la fiesta y viva la familia: Long live fiesta and long live the family

Bibliography

¡Flamenco!; Haas, Ken and Gwynne Edwards; Thames and Hudson, Ltd.; London, 2000.

Flamenco: The Art of Flamenco, Its History and Development until our Days; Thiel-Cramer, Barbara; Remark AB; Lidingo, Sweden; 1990.

Flamenco Spirit, 'Becoming the Dance'; Morca, Teodoro; Kendall/Hunt Publishing Company; Dubuque, Iowa; 1990.

Acknowledgments:

MUCHAS GRACIAS…to my friend, Beverly, who was willing to take a risk with me in this project, giving her time and talents to understand and illustrate the story…to my son, Matthew Struven, for using his editing skills to comb through my manuscript…to my husband, Mike Struven, for helping me with the HTML formatting of the book…to my neighbor, Valerie Vampola, who gave me an interview and loaned me props for my author photo…to Dr. Chela Sandoval, Chican@ Studies Professor at UCSB, for her sensitive critique of the manuscript…to my sister, Laurie Vengoechea, for producing my author photo…and—last but not least—to all the teachers and students of the Santa Barbara and Goleta dance studios that provide us with entertainment year after year with their skill, passion, *aire y gracia*! —CVS

About the Illustrator:

Since she was 10 years old, Beverly Womack has pursued innumerable white spaces on which to pour out her illustrations and calligraphy. Trained and experienced in graphic design, her interests are multi-faceted, from logo design to framed verse. It was only a matter of time that she would arrive in the book-making arena to express her versatility of style and excellence of skill. Beverly lives in Southern California. She teaches calligraphy in elementary and high schools, public libraries, and in her home.

About the Author:

Cyndi Struven was in fifth grade when she began writing mystery stories for her sisters to read. After a long hiatus, she began writing in her free time as a stay-at-home mom. When not writing, Cyndi works as a substitute librarian in local schools, loves to volunteer, hike, run on the beach with her dog, and solve puzzles.

73826808R00024

Made in the USA
San Bernardino, CA
10 April 2018